Doc

Sleepy

Mrs. L. Honeychurch

Book Club Edition

First American Edition. Copyright © 1979 by The Walt Disney Company.
All rights reserved under International and Pan-American Copyright Conventions.
Published in the United States by Random House, Inc., New York, and simultaneously in Canada by Random House
of Canada Limited, Toronto. Originally published in Denmark as DE 7 SMÅ DVAERGE OG SNEHVIDES.
DIAMANT by Gutenberghus Bladene, Copenhagen.
ISBN: 0-394-84356-8 (trade),   ISBN: 0-394-94356-2 (lib. bdg.)
Manufactured in the United States of America
E F G H I J K

WALT DISNEY'S

Snow White
Visits the
Seven Dwarfs

Random House 🏠 New York

It was early morning in the forest.
The seven dwarfs were going to work
in the diamond mine.

They sang as they marched along:
"Hi ho! Hi ho!
It's off to work we go!"

Suddenly their friend
Bluebird appeared.
He had something important
to tell them.

The dwarfs stopped to listen.
"Good news," said Bluebird. "I have
just come from Snow White's castle."

"How is
Snow White?"
asked Doc,
the leader of the dwarfs.

"She is well," said
Bluebird. "She and
the Prince are coming
to the forest
this afternoon
to visit you."

"That is wonderful!" said
he dwarf named Happy.

"We have not seen her
a long time," said
rumpy. "We should do
omething special for her."

Everyone agreed with him.

The dwarfs worked happily that day because
they knew that Snow White was coming for a visit.

But they could not think of anything special
to do for her.

Then Dopey found a big, beautiful diamond.

"We will give it to Snow White
as a present," said Doc.
Even Grumpy agreed
it was the perfect gift
for their friend.

The dwarfs stopped
work early that day.
Dopey carried
the diamond proudly
as they all marched
home.

They sang together:
"*Hi ho! Hi ho!*
It's home from work we go!"

When the dwarfs opened the door of their
cottage, they saw there was work to do.
They had left their little house a mess.

Things were out of place.
There were dirty dishes
everywhere.

They wanted the house
to be clean for Snow White.

So Sleepy
swept the stairs.

Dopey piled up
the dirty dishes...

and Doc
washed them.

A squirrel and
a little bird
dusted the corners.

Grumpy mopped
the floors and
made them shine.

Doc cooked a delicious dinner.
Dopey and his friends picked flowers
for the table.

"Now we are ready," said Doc. "Dopey,
you put the diamond at Snow White's place
at the table."

But where *was* the diamond?

No one seemed to know.

Now, after all their hard work, they could not find their gift for Snow White.

"You had it last,"
Sneezy said to Happy.
"I did not," said
Happy. "*You* did!"

Grumpy pointed a finger
at Bashful.

"I bet *you* lost it, Bashful,"
he said grumpily.

But they knew
the only thing
to do was
to look for
the diamond.

They searched high...and low.

But they could not
find the diamond.

Suddenly Bluebird
appeared.

"Snow White and the Prince
are on their way," he said.
"They will be here soon."

"Oh no!" cried Doc.
"What are we going
to do? We had
a beautiful diamond
for Snow White...."

"And now
it is gone,"
said Grumpy.

"Bluebird,
can you help
us?" asked Sleepy.

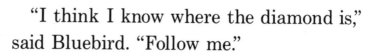

"I think I know where the diamond is,"
said Bluebird. "Follow me."

Off they went, with Bluebird in the lead.
He flew to a tall tree
where an angry old
magpie had a nest.

Something in
the nest was sparkling.

They knew it was the diamond.

"You give us back our diamond!"
Doc said to the magpie.

But
the magpie
did not
move.

The dwarfs
stood on
each other's
shoulders to get
the diamond.

Sleepy was
at the top.

But he
did not dare
reach for
the diamond.

He was
afraid of
the angry
magpie.

Finally Bluebird and his friends
swooped down and chased
the magpie away from the nest.

"I have it!"
said Sleepy
as he held up
the diamond.

Suddenly Sneezy went "AH-CHOO!"

All the dwarfs came tumbling down.
Sleepy landed on top of the pile.
He was still holding the sparkling jewel.

"Let us hurry!" said Bluebird.
"Snow White and the Prince
will reach the cottage
any minute."

The little men ran
down the path.

Doc held on to the diamond while his friend
the deer gave him a ride.

They reached the cottage
before Snow White.

Dopey put the diamond
carefully on the table.

Then Snow White and the Prince arrived
in their royal carriage.
The dwarfs bowed before their honored guests.
Snow White and the Prince bowed, too.

They went inside for dinner.

"Everything looks lovely," said Snow White.
"And what a beautiful diamond!"

"It is for you, Snow White," said the dwarfs.

Snow White thanked them
and gave them each a kiss.

After dinner,
three of
the dwarfs
played
lively music.

Snow White danced
with the Prince.
Then she danced with
the dwarfs.
The hours flew by.

It was very late when Snow White and
the Prince went home to the castle.
The dwarfs waved good-by to them
as they rode away.

"What a wonderful night,"
said the dwarfs as they climbed into bed.
"I am glad we did something
special for dear Snow White," said Doc.
The dwarfs all nodded
and closed their sleepy eyes.

Bashful

Sneezy

Happ[y]

Dopey

Grumpy